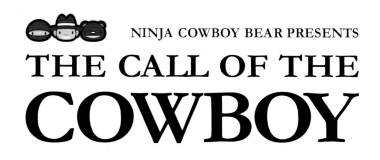

NINJA COWBOY BEAR PRESENTS

THE CALL OF THE
COWBOY

For Mom and Dad — D.B.
To Riley, Taylor and Jacob Galloway — H.L.

Kids Can Press acknowledges the financial support of the Government of Ontario, through the
Ontario Media Development Corporation's Ontario Book Initiative; the Ontario Arts Council;
the Canada Council for the Arts; and the Government of Canada, through the BPIDP, for our
publishing activity.

Published in Canada by
Kids Can Press Ltd.
25 Dockside Drive
Toronto, ON M5A 0B5

Published in the U.S. by
Kids Can Press Ltd.
2250 Military Road
Tonawanda, NY 14150

www.kidscanpress.com

The text in this book is set in Garamond.

Edited by Yvette Ghione
Designed by Hilary Leung

This book is smyth sewn casebound.
Manufactured in Singapore, in 3/2011 by Tien Wah Press (Pte) Ltd.

CM 11 0 9 8 7 6 5 4 3 2 1

The Japanese characters on page 19 are pronounced "Fu N!" The expression can be translated as
"Hmph!" The bird call "Piyo! Piyo! Piyo!" on page 28 can be translated as "Cheep! Cheep! Cheep!"

www.ninja-cowboy-bear.com

Library and Archives Canada Cataloguing in Publication

Bruins, David
    Ninja Cowboy Bear presents The call of the cowboy /
David Bruins and Hilary Leung.

ISBN 978-1-55453-748-8

I. Leung, Hilary II. Title. III. Title: Call of the cowboy.

PS8603.R835N55 2011   jC813'.6   C2011-900082-2

Kids Can Press is a **Corus** Entertainment company

NINJA COWBOY BEAR PRESENTS

THE CALL OF THE
COWBOY

David Bruins and Hilary Leung

Kids Can Press

The cowboy was a good friend to the ninja and the bear.

He was kind.

He was caring.

He was fun.

He was funny.

But sometimes he could cause a ruckus.

One day his noisiness came
between him and his friends …

And here is what happened.

The bear was going out to photograph birds.
The cowboy went along, too.

But the bear was not having any success, so he decided to call it quits. He told the cowboy that it was not a good day for photographs.

The cowboy was confused. He saw lots of birds flying around.

So the cowboy decided to see what the ninja was doing.

The ninja was reading a book. The cowboy sat down to read, too.

But the ninja was not turning many pages, so he decided to call it quits. He told the cowboy his book was not very interesting.

The cowboy was confused. He thought that book was terrific.

ふん！

The cowboy wondered why his friends were acting so strangely.
Did they not enjoy his company?

As he walked along, the cowboy tried to understand.
But he could not concentrate.

Until he came to a quiet place.

Then the cowboy understood perfectly.

Meanwhile, the bear had returned
to his photography.

He took lots of
photographs this time.

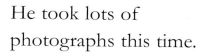

He could not wait to show
them to the cowboy.

Similarly, the ninja had
resumed reading his book.

He turned many pages this time, and
soon he had read the whole book.

He could not wait to share
the story with the cowboy.

The bear and the ninja found the cowboy singing a quiet song.
They asked if they could keep him company.

The bear shared his photographs,
and they all did their best bird calls.

The ninja shared his story,
and they all howled with laughter.

Then the cowboy asked his friends if
they would accompany him in song.

And together they made a wonderful racket.